D1622334

GLITTERFIES THE GALA

created by
JAY ALBEE

STONE ARCH BOOKS
a capstone imprint

Published by Stone Arch Books, an imprint of Capstone
1710 Roe Crest Drive, North Mankato, Minnesota 56003
capstonepub.com

Library of Congress Cataloging-in-Publication Data is available
on the Library of Congress website
ISBN: 9781666344073 (hardcover)
ISBN: 9781666344110 (paperback)
ISBN: 9781666344158 (ebook PDF)

Summary: Riley and their friends help throw a fundraiser to fix
the elevator at the local library.

Special thanks to Manu Shadow Velasco for their consultation.

Designed by Nathan Gassman

TABLE OF CONTENTS

CHAPTER ONE
A PROFESSIONAL FESTOONER 8

CHAPTER TWO
THAT'S ONE WAY TO AVOID AN OVERDUE FINE 14

CHAPTER THREE
EMPLOYEES ONLY IN THE LIBRARY OF THINGS 22

CHAPTER FOUR
A BOX THAT BOOMS. 28

CHAPTER FIVE
DOWNSTAIRS IS WHERE THEY KEEP THE NAPKINS, CUPS, AND GHOSTS. 34

CHAPTER SIX
THE PEOPLE MAKE THE PARTY. 40

CHAPTER SEVEN
SAMOSAS AND SECRET STRANGERS. 48

CHAPTER EIGHT
MYSTERY (ENVELOPES) SOLVED 54

I'M RILEY!

I LOVE SO MANY THINGS! I LOVE CRAFTING.

THE ONLY THING BETTER THAN MAKING MESSES IS MAKING COOL STUFF.

I LOVE MY PARENTS, MY COUSINS, AND MY FRIENDS.

I LOVE DOGS AND CATS . . .

AND BIRDS AND FISH . . .

AND DRAGONS AND UNICORNS AND ALL ANIMALS!

I'M NONBINARY, AND I LOVE THAT TOO. I DON'T HAVE TO BE A BOY OR A GIRL.

I CAN JUST BE ME!

MX. AUDE TEACHES HELPFUL TERMS

Cisgender: Cisgender (or cis) people identify with the gender written on their birth certificate. They are usually boys or girls.

Gender identity: Regardless of the gender written on a person's birth certificate, they decide their gender identity. It might change over time. A person's interests, clothes, and behavior might be traditionally associated with their gender identity, or they might not.

Honorific: Young people use honorifics when they talk to or about adults, especially teachers. Mr. is the honorific for a man, Mrs. or Ms. for a woman, and Mx. is the gender-neutral honorific often used for nonbinary people. It is pronounced "mix." Nonbinary people may also use Mr., Mrs., or Ms. as well.

LGBTQ+: This stands for lesbian, gay, bisexual (also pansexual), transgender, queer. There are lots of ways people describe their gender and attraction. These are just a few of those ways. The + sign means that there are many, many more, and they are all included in the acronym LGBTQ+.

Nonbinary: Nonbinary people have a gender identity other than boy or girl. They may be neither, both, a combination, or sometimes one and sometimes the other.

Pronouns: Pronouns are how people refer to themselves and others (she/her, they/them, he/him, etc.). Pronouns often line up with gender identity (especially for cis people), but not always. It's best to ask a person what pronouns they like to use.

Queer: An umbrella term for people who identify as LGBTQ+.

Transgender: Transgender (or trans) people do not identify with the gender listed on their birth certificate. They might identify as the other binary gender, both genders, or another gender identity.

CHAPTER ONE

A PROFESSIONAL FESTOONER

The library where Mama worked was a small neighborhood branch. It was an old three-story building, wedged between a dry cleaner's and a tiny park.

The library wasn't usually open on Sundays, but Mama, Riley, and Dad had been there since the morning. They were prepping for a party that night.

The library was having a fundraising gala with food and drinks and stuff to buy at a silent auction. A silent auction was where people wrote down what they would pay for something without seeing how much anybody else had written down. The highest bid would win. It could be very exciting!

The big item for the silent auction was Dad's painting for the cover of the next Throne of Flame and Truth book. The book was called *Allegra and the Dragon*. The books were written by famous, private author L. L. Lamar. Dad did all the covers. When Dad painted this one, he had Riley wear a crown and hold a sword so he could take reference photos. Now the painting stood propped up on a table in the middle of the library. It looked spectacular! Riley was sure it would raise a ton of money.

Riley had made decorations to match the theme of the painting. There were paper flags, shimmery green dragon scales, and golden jewels. Crepe paper streamers hung from the banisters, bookshelves, and doorknobs.

Riley hung extra streamers and construction paper stars on the closed elevator doors. They thought the elevator should be absolutely covered in decorations—or festooned. *Festooned* was a word Riley had heard recently. And that's how they wanted the elevator doors to look.

Everyone needed to remember that the whole reason for the gala was to raise enough money to fix the broken elevator. Riley made a sign that said: OUT OF ORDER (so please donate!)

Riley stepped back from their work on the elevator and smiled. They were happy with how festooned it was. It was definitely the first thing that people would see when they arrived. Then Riley wondered if the most festooned thing should be the *Allegra and the Dragon* painting. Should *that* be the first thing that people saw when they arrived so they remembered to bid in the auction? Before Riley could decide, their best friends Lea and Cricket arrived with Lea's mom. They were going to help set up for the gala too.

"Riley!" Lea called from the door. "The elevator looks so good!"

"And look at your dad's painting!" added Cricket. "Wow!"

Riley beamed. Question answered: everything was just right.

CHAPTER TWO

THAT'S ONE WAY TO AVOID AN OVERDUE FINE

Lea and Cricket had arrived just in time. Riley had run out of things to do. And Paola was going to arrive soon. Paola was the other librarian at this branch. Riley really did not want to see her today.

Lea's mom carried a big tote bag to where Mama was setting up another table, just to the side of Dad's painting. Lea's mom had brought a dozen adorable dragons of different sizes that she had knitted or crocheted. They would be in the auction too.

"Did you make any of those dragons, Lea?" asked Riley.

Lea gave Riley a look like "have we met?" and shook her head, laughing.

"Mom made most of them on the sidelines of my games and practices the last few weeks."

"They look great!" said Cricket. "I know my stepmom will bid on a bunch for sure."

Cricket had four younger half-siblings, and they would love the dragon toys.

Lea looked around. "You know, it feels weird being in the library when it's closed."

"I was thinking the same thing," agreed Cricket.

"It does?" asked Riley.

They looked around too. Riley was here all the time when the library was closed. They went with their dad when he picked up Mama after work. They would wait around for her to finish up.

Riley tried to imagine what it would be like if they'd never seen the library like this—quiet and empty and with only half the lights on.

"Yeah, it's like seeing a teacher at the supermarket," laughed Lea.

"Or seeing your neighborhood on the news," added Cricket.

Riley laughed. "I get that," they said.

Just then, Paola came into the library, pushing a cart full of soda and champagne.

"The library looks great!" she said as she bustled in. "Oh, you decided to set up the tables like that? I was thinking a slight angle might have more *pop*." She did a "pop" motion with her hands.

Mama had been working with Paola a long time and knew that Paola could spend hours on getting the angle of the table just right. But Mama had been planning this gala for weeks, and she'd been working hard all day. Riley knew when Mama was in business mode, no one could change her focus—not even Paola.

Mama said, "Maybe we can think about that later? First we need to set up the drinks tables, get the cash box ready, and hang up these other items for the auction."

"Right!" said Paola, with the full force of her enthusiasm. "I'm on it! Just a few more loads to come in from my trunk! Oh, hi, Riley!"

Riley waved at Paola and quickly tugged Lea and Cricket toward the stairs at the back of the room.

"Come on, I'll show you some of the out-of-bounds stuff."

"Awesome," breathed Lea, kind of nervously, following Riley as they dashed up the half-lit stairs to the second floor.

"Hold up," Cricket said once he'd caught up. "What just happened? Are you avoiding Paola?"

"Ugh," Riley said. "No. Maybe. Okay, yes, I am." Riley sighed. "I have an overdue library book, and I don't want to get in trouble."

"Oof," said Lea. "Paola is so intense about overdue books."

"Right?" agreed Riley.

"Once she threatened to suspend my library card," said Lea.

"Why don't you just return it?" asked Cricket.

"I can't find it!" Riley said. "And I'm out of renewals."

"Ah," said Lea and Cricket together.

"I've just got to avoid her until I find the book. It has to be somewhere. Anyway, come check this out," said Riley, leading Lea and Cricket through the stacks of the dark second floor to a closed door.

"Riley, this door says 'Employees Only,'" whispered Lea. "We're not supposed to go in here."

"I know," Riley whispered back and opened the door.

CHAPTER THREE

EMPLOYEES ONLY IN THE LIBRARY OF THINGS

"What is this place?" asked Lea.

"It's the Library of Things," replied Riley, smiling.

"Woah," said Lea and Cricket.

They stepped into the room. It was as neatly organized as the rest of the library, but all the shelves and cubby holes were full of things instead of books.

Riley explained, "It's stuff that isn't books that you can borrow from the library."

In the kitchen section, Lea held up a hook-shaped attachment for a stand mixer.

"What's this?" she asked.

"What does the label say?" asked Riley.

"Um, 'dough hook.'" Lea looked at the dough hook. "But what does it do?"

"Who knows!" said Riley. "I don't know what half this stuff is!"

Lea picked up the next item on the shelf and read, "Sausage-making attachment."

"Ooh," said Riley. "I've never seen that one! It's always checked out." Riley looked over the white plastic funnel with a short tube on the end.

From another part of the room, Cricket said, "Hey! We can use this green screen for our explorers project! We can climb a mountain and dive under the sea!"

Cricket was making the *beep boop* sounds he made when he was excited. "*Boop boop!* This project will be so fun!"

"What's the last thing you borrowed from here?" Lea asked Riley. "There's so much to pick from!"

Riley pointed out a briefcase of polished leather with shining clasps. "I carried my paint set around in it for a week." Lea and Cricket laughed.

The friends ran around the cramped stacks shouting out what they were finding:

"A bubble machine!"

"Fourteen wigs! No, fifteen!"

"Ice-cream maker!"

"Ukulele! Accordion! Bongos! Kazoo!"

"A human skeleton? What?!"

"It's a plastic cast," Riley said. "I promise it's not a real one. I checked."

"Oh," said Cricket, a little disappointed.

"Hey," said Lea. "Come check this out!"

Cricket and Riley rushed to Lea. Cricket said, "*Beep boop beep!*"

Lea had found a boombox, huge and silver. There was a box of cassette tapes in the cubby hole too.

Riley grinned wide. "Just what every party needs."

Suddenly, the door to the Library of Things burst open.

"Ah, Riley, here you are," said Paola from the doorway. Riley gulped.

"Oh, hi, Paola," said Riley.

Paola said, "Riley, I—"

"Sorry, Paola, can't talk. I've got to bring this stuff to Mama." Riley, Lea, and Cricket bustled past Paola, who held the door open for them.

CHAPTER FOUR

A BOX THAT BOOMS

Riley and their friends took their findings to the first level. The drinks table had been set up, ready to sell to a crowd. At least, they hoped it would be a crowd.

The library really needed an elevator that didn't trap people inside it once a week. And it wasn't right that the people who got trapped the most were the ones who couldn't make it up and down the stairs.

On a big whiteboard, Dad had drawn a border in erasable marker. Vines were intertwined with flowers, little dragons, crowns, and swords. Mama and Lea's mom were taping sealed envelopes to it. Some of the envelopes had the name of what was inside, like a voucher to a local restaurant, a promise that Dad would paint a pet portrait, or a week of free classes at the yoga center.

Some of the envelopes just had question marks on them. People would bid on them in the silent auction without knowing what they were or what they were worth. Riley had a few dollars to bid on a mystery prize. What if it was a pony ride, free pizza for a month, or a bright green frog in its very own terrarium?

"Dad! Mama! Look what we found!" Riley yelled.

Dad grinned at the discovery.

Mama laughed and hugged Riley. "Amazing. What's a party without music?"

"That's what I said," said Riley.

"Are you three staying out of trouble?" asked Lea's mom.

"Yep," they all replied, and it wasn't even a lie, really.

Dad flipped through the tapes. "Holy cats," he said, "there are some solid gold tunes in here. Let's get this party started!"

He slipped a tape into the boombox and winked at Mama. As soon as the first notes filled the room, Mama smiled wide. Riley did too. This was one of Mama's favorites. She danced every time she heard it. Now she put her hands in the air and flicked her hips. In the next moment, everyone was dancing along.

When the next song started, Mama, still dancing, went back to taping up envelopes. Riley saw that Mama was still focused, but with every beat, business mode was melting away. She turned to Riley, Lea, and Cricket. "Can you three run downstairs and grab napkins and cups?"

"Sure, Mama."

"Posthaste!" added Mama.

Postehaste was a funny thing Mama said when she meant "right now" but wasn't cranky about it. Riley bounced down the basement steps with Lea and Cricket close behind.

When Mama was dancing, the party was definitely started!

DOWNSTAIRS IS WHERE THEY KEEP THE NAPKINS, CUPS, AND GHOSTS

Downstairs was a storage area. There were windows high up that showed people's feet as they walked past the library, and, best of all, the dogs they were walking.

34

Riley flipped the light switch but only one light came on. That happened all the time. The next library fundraiser should be to fix the downstairs wiring.

Riley didn't like coming down here alone. There was something spooky about the way the concrete stayed so cold. And it was so quiet. They were glad to have Cricket and Lea there with them.

"Come on," said Riley. "Everything is in the cupboard over here."

Cricket followed Riley into the gloomy cellar. Lea stayed at the base of the stairs, in the light spilling down from the floor above. She said, "Actually, I'm going to stay here. I'm a bit scared of the dark. Not, like, afraid of it. But not *not* afraid, either."

"There's nothing to worry about," said Cricket.

"I know that," replied Lea, "but knowing doesn't change how I feel."

"It's okay, Lea," said Riley. "Stay there. We'll toss the packet of napkins to you!"

Lea laughed. "Okay!"

At the cupboard, Riley passed sleeves of cups to Cricket. Riley picked up a packet of napkins and was about to throw it across the cellar to Lea, when they heard Lea yelp in fright followed by a second, squeakier yelp.

"Lea!" called Riley, rushing back to the stairs. "Are you okay?"

There, Riley and Cricket found Lea— and Nelle. Nelle was a very shy second grader, and Riley's neighbor. The second yelp had come from Nelle!

Nelle gulped and said, "Your parents said you were down here, and I came to help." Being shy, she had moved quietly. Lea didn't know she was there until Nelle touched Lea's arm. Now, Nelle and Lea shook with laughter.

"You okay?" asked Riley, who couldn't really tell if the shock was wearing off or sinking in.

"Yeah," gasped Lea, "I think so." She took Nelle's hand, and they laughed even harder.

"Here, take these." Riley handed Nelle a package of napkins and Lea two sleeves of cups from their overloaded arms.

Then Mama's voice came down the stairs. "Riley, do you have those cups?"

"Coming, Mama!" Riley shouted. They all dashed up the stairs.

CHAPTER SIX

THE PEOPLE MAKE THE PARTY

Cricket and Lea took the cups out and set them up as fast as Paola could pour drinks. There were already dozens of grown-ups filling the tiny library space and more coming in through the doors.

Lea's mom was taking money and calling out drink orders. Riley didn't know how much it cost to fix an elevator, but they were definitely on their way!

"Thanks, kids!" said Paola. "And Riley, don't go home tonight before I get a chance to talk to you, okay?"

"Sure," Riley said as they ducked away.

They found Mama and Dad, supervising the silent auction. The auction was really busy, which was awesome. And some people were already making song requests at the music station.

"Mama, do you need anything else?" Riley asked.

Mama gave Riley a quick hug, "Thanks, Ry. Go grab me an empanada, would you?"

"I'll help," said Nelle, who was still by Riley's elbow.

Riley and Nelle shuffled and squeezed through the crowd. The party didn't have a dress code, but Riley could tell that people had made an effort. It was a beautiful evening. There was art and drinks, and the party was called a gala! If that didn't make it feel special and worth putting on fancy clothes, then Riley didn't know what would.

Outside, Nelle's mom and dad were selling empanadas, tamales, and samosas out of their food truck. They were donating all the money they made that night to the elevator repair. Nelle and Riley stood in line. The line was long but moving quickly. They talked about which mystery envelope seemed like it might have the most interesting prize. Soon enough they were at the front.

"Riley!" Nelle's mom beamed. "How's it all going inside?"

"Good, I think. There are lots of people," Riley said.

"Lots," agreed Nelle, who could get nervous in crowds.

"Stick with me, Nelle, and let me know if you need to go somewhere quiet for a bit. I know all the best spots," Riley said.

"Thanks, Riley," said Nelle.

"Three empanadas, please."

"And one for me," added Nelle. She never got sick of her parents' empanadas.

Riley took out some money, but Nelle's dad waved it away.

"Tonight, you eat for free!" he said. Nelle's mom handed Riley two samosas and a tamale as well.

"Thanks, Mr. and Mrs. Jackson," said Riley, then headed back inside.

"Thanks, Ry," said Mama and Dad when Riley handed over the empanadas. "You can share the rest with your friends."

Riley picked the mystery envelope they wanted to bid on and Mama carefully wrote the envelope's number down. Then Riley and Nelle went to find Lea and Cricket.

On the way through the crowd, Riley found their neighbor, Toby. Toby was a grandma who had been trapped in the elevator last week. She was a huge fan of the Throne of Flame and Truth series and told Riley the story of every book just right, because Riley was too young to read them yet. She was standing in front of the painting, soaking in all its details.

"I just want to stand here and look at this painting until the next book comes out," Toby said with a happy sigh.

CHAPTER SEVEN

SAMOSAS AND SECRET STRANGERS

Lea and Cricket were sitting on the stairs to the second floor, where they had a view of the whole party. Riley and Nelle sat down next to them. Cricket's stomach rumbled.

He looked at Nelle's empanada and said, "Wow, that smells good."

Riley handed him a samosa, "Dairy-free vegetarian for you."

They handed Lea a tamale, "Gluten-free for you."

Then, taking a big bite of an empanada, Riley said, "And yummers for me."

Over happy, steaming bites, the friends looked out over the party. The room was so full that the door had to be propped open and the party spilled out onto the sidewalk. The smell of the Jacksons' good food wafted in on the warm night air.

"Now the library feels even more different," said Lea.

Riley realized she was right. They had always felt that even when it was empty the library was full of life. It was full of stories and facts and stuff like dough hooks and briefcases. But now the library was filled with chatting and laughing and music.

"And, I mean, we're usually not allowed to eat in here."

"Yeah," agreed Riley. "It's great."

"Look, there's Mx. Aude and Mr. Lane," said Cricket, pointing out their teacher and school librarian.

"It's weird seeing your teachers all dressed up at the library!" laughed Lea.

Riley saw Dad, trapped in a corner by Paola. Riley knew what she was asking him about. Paola was sure that Dad knew the plot of the next Throne of Flame and Truth book, even though he didn't.

Dad pointed out another person in the crowd, who was wearing a nice jacket and standing near Riley. Riley watched Paola push her way through the crowd toward the stranger. She stuck out her hand and started talking immediately.

"Hello! I'm Paola. I was just talking to my friend about the Throne of Flame and Truth series. He does the cover art for it, like the painting there with the dragon and Allegra and the mountain. It's my favorite series! My friend said that you were the person to talk to about it," Paola said.

After a moment, Riley decided that Paola had meant the stranger was the person to talk *at* about it. The stranger couldn't get a word in.

Eventually, Paola had to pause for a breath, and the stranger said quickly, "It was so nice to meet you, Paola. I just have to do something . . . excuse me," and slipped away into the crowd. Riley chuckled. It looked like they weren't the only one avoiding Paola tonight!

Riley watched as the stranger made eye contact with Dad across the room. The stranger made a pretend mad face and Dad winked. Huh, so Dad knew the stranger. Riley wondered who he was.

MYSTERY (ENVELOPES) SOLVED

Soon it was time for the auction winners to be announced. Dad cut the music so Mama could read out the winners. People cheered when they won a voucher envelope or knew someone who had. There was lots of cheering. Cricket's stepmom won four of Lea's mom's knitted dragons.

They were going to do the mystery envelopes last, and Riley was nervous-excited. But first, the big *Allegra and the Dragon* painting.

"The highest bidder for this very special artwork is . . ." Mama checked her list and called out, "Lew Lamar!"

The whole room—and those peeking in through the open door—gasped.

Lea, Cricket, and Nelle asked, "Who's Lew Lamar?"

"L. L. Lamar! He's the writer. The author. He writes the Throne of Flame and Truth series!" whispered Riley.

If Lea, Cricket, and Nelle reacted, it was lost in the hubbub of the room. The room was loud with astonishment and guesses about who might be the famous writer.

Mama waved her hands around and Dad did his loudest whistle to quiet everyone down. "Lew has a few words."

Then the stranger in the nice jacket who had been cornered by Paola stepped up next to Dad and faced the room. The audience clapped and cheered.

"Thank you," Lew Lamar said. "It is my great and humble honor to donate the painting to this library, for everyone to enjoy."

But that wasn't all. Lew Lamar was pleased to announce that all the mystery envelopes were prizes that he had donated—things like signed books, voicemail messages, and even a lunch. The crowd erupted into gasps of excitement, even as Riley let out a sigh of disappointment. Not a pony ride or free pizza or a frog after all. They didn't even really mind when someone else won the envelope they had bid for. The winner, Mr. Bamber from a few blocks over, was thrilled with his prize.

Mama announced that they had raised enough money to fix the elevator. Everyone cheered, Dad turned the music up again, and the whole room became a dance floor.

Soon enough, all the empanadas were eaten, all the drinks were gone, and all the dances were danced. What a night!

The only people left were the clean-up crew: Mama, Dad, Riley, Lea, Cricket, and Paola.

Riley, Cricket, and Lea filled big black bags with napkins, cups, and crepe paper streamers for the recycling pickup. Riley tried to always keep a bag and one of their friends between themself and Paola. But being vigilant was tiring, and it had been a long day. Riley only let their guard down for a second.

"I've been trying to catch you all night!" said Paola, standing right next to Riley.

Riley was taking the streamers and stars off the elevator. There was nowhere to hide!

Riley sighed, slumped a little, and said, "Oh, Paola. I'm sorry! I know, I know. *The Age of the Dinosaurs* is overdue and I'm out of renewals. I'll bring it back soon, I promise!"

Paola looked surprised for a beat, then confused.

Cricket said, "That's the book you've been worried about? Riley, you loaned it to me last time I was at your house. I brought it back to the library days ago. On time!" Cricket laughed.

"I did?" asked Riley. "You did?" Cricket nodded.

Riley's face brightened, "Oh! Okay then!" Riley looked at Paola. "I'm so relieved! If I don't have an overdue library book, what did you want to talk to me about?"

"I wanted to ask if you would teach me how to make these stars you hung on the elevator," said Paola. "My son is getting engaged and I think these would be wonderful decorations for his party!"

Riley laughed, more at themself than anything that was actually funny, and said, "Of course, Paola, that sounds fun."

In no time, Mama and Paola agreed that the library was clean. Riley proudly added one more sign to the elevator, smiled, and headed home. What a night!

THE END

DISCUSSION QUESTIONS

1. Why do you think it's so important to fix the elevator in the library?

2. Riley avoids Paola because they don't want to get in trouble for an overdue library book. Was this a good way for Riley to solve their problem? Why or why not?

3. Do you think the gala was a good idea for a fundraiser? What kind of fundraiser would you like to go to?

WRITING PROMPTS

1. Pretend that you won a mystery envelope at the silent auction. Write about what you got and how you feel about it.

2. Everyone has fears. Lea is a little afraid of the dark. What are you scared of? Write a list of things you can do to face one of your fears.

3. Pretend you get to stay overnight in the library for a night. Write about your adventure.

MEET THE CREATORS

Jay Albee is the joint pen name for LGBTQ+ couple Jen Breach and J. Anthony. Between them they've done lots of jobs: archaeologist, illustrator, ticket taker, and bagel baker, but now they write and draw all day long in their row house in South Philadelphia, Pennsylvania.

At a party, you'll find Jen and J. out on the dance floor.

Jen Breach

J. Anthony